First published in hardback in Great Britain by Andersen Press Ltd in 2005
First published in paperback by HarperCollins Children's Books in 2007
5 7 9 10 8 6 4

ISBN-13: 978-0-00-721491-4
ISBN-10: 0-00-721491-X

HarperCollins Children's Books is a division of HarperCollins Publishers Ltd.

Text and illustrations copyright © Tony Ross 2005, 2007

Visit our website at: www.harpercollinschildrensbooks.co.uk

Printed and bound by Printing Express, Hong Kong

I Want A Friend

Tony Ross

HarperCollins *Children's Books*

"He doesn't want to play with me!"
wailed the Little Princess.

"He only does boys' stuff."

"Never mind," said the Queen. "You start school tomorrow. You'll have lots of friends to play with there."

Next day at school, the Little Princess put her
hat and coat on her peg...

...and went to play with the other children.

Molly and Polly were skipping.
"We don't want to play with YOU," they said.

When Agnes came along, the Little Princess smiled.
"I don't want to play with YOU!" said Agnes.

"Can I play with you?" asked the Little Princess.
"No!" said Willy, and he went to play with
Molly, Polly and Agnes.

The Little Princess stood sadly by herself.
Then she saw another new girl standing by herself.

"Nobody will play with me," said the Little Princess.
"Nor with me," said the other girl.

There were lots of children standing by themselves.
"Nobody will play with us," said the Little Princess.
"Or us!" said the lots of children.

The Little Princess and all the other children
with no friends shared their sweets and fruit.
"I wish I had a friend," they all said.

They all played Tag together.
"It would be more fun if we had some friends,"
they all said.

In the classroom, all the children with no friends sat together. Some other children with no friends joined in.

"Don't worry about having no friends," said the
Little Princess to the other new girl. "I haven't
got any either. It's not so bad."
"It's not so bad," said all the others.

At going-home time, all the children with no friends helped each other with their coats and hats.

When the Little Princess put on her hat, Molly, Polly, Agnes and Willy gasped: "GOSH, SHE'S A PRINCESS!"

The Little Princess turned to all the other children
with no friends. "Would you like to come home
to tea?" she said.

"Yes, please," they said.

"Can we come, too?" said Molly, Polly, Agnes and Willy.

The Little Princess frowned her terrible frown.

"All right," she said. "Come on."

"Goodness!" said the Queen.
"Who are all these children?"

"My friends," said the Little Princess.

Collect all the funny stories featuring the demanding Little Princess!

 978-0-00-723621-3

 I Want To Be — Tony Ross — 978-0-00-724282-5

 I Want My Dinner — Tony Ross — 978-0-00-723620-6

 I Want A Sister — Tony Ross — 978-0-00-724281-8

 I Don't Want To Go To Hospital — Tony Ross  978-0-00-710957-9

 I Want My Dummy — Tony Ross — 978-0-00-724283-2

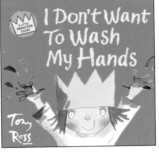 I Don't Want To Wash My Hands — Tony Ross — 978-0-00-715072-4

 I Want My Tooth — Tony Ross — 978-0-00-724365-5

 I Don't Want To Go To Bed — Tony Ross — 978-0-00-719478-0

 I Want My Mum — Tony Ross — 978-0-00-720033-7

 I Want A Friend — Tony Ross — 978-0-00-721491-4

"The Little Princess has huge appeal to toddlers and Tony Ross's illustrations are brilliantly witty."
Practical Parenting

Tony Ross was born in London in 1938. His dream was to work with horses but instead he went to art college in Liverpool. Since then, Tony has worked as an art director at an advertising agency, a graphic designer, a cartoonist, a teacher and a film maker – as well as illustrating over 250 books! Tony, his wife Zoe and family live in Macclesfield, Cheshire.

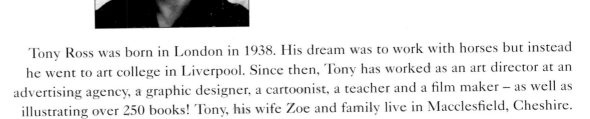